Bugs Bunny™

D0654004

TITLES AVAILABLE IN BUZZ BOOKS

First published 1990 by Buzz Books,
an imprint of the Octopus Publishing Group,
Michelin House, 81 Fulham Road, London SW3 6RB

LONDON   MELBOURNE   AUCKLAND

ISBN 1 85591 017 9

Printed and bound in the UK by BPCC Paulton Books Ltd

Bugs Bunny

IN

KNiGHTY KNiGHT BUGS

TM.

Story by Norman Redfern

based on an original cartoon

Illustrations by CLIC!

Hi, Bugs Bunny here. Do you remember the legend of King Arthur, who had a special table made for his knights? It was round, so that no-one could sit at the head of it and boss the others around, and most important, they could all reach the ketchup.

> ONE OF YE KNIGHTS MUST RECOVER THE SINGING SWORD...

> BUT THE BLACK KNIGHT IS INVINCIBLE!

> BUT THE BLACK KNIGHT HAS A FIRE BREATHING DRAGON!

SIR LOIN OF BEEF

SIR OSIS OF LIVER

One day , the King announced that ever since the Black Knight had captured their magic Singing Sword, their luck had turned bad. The knights were bold, they knew no fear, but they were afraid of the dark and the Black Knight scared the living daylights out of them.

In those days I was the Court Jester. My job was to put King Arthur back in the pink when he was feeling blue, browned off or green at the gills. I told him that rescuing the sword was a fool's errand. He agreed, and pointed out that since I was the Fool, I could do the errand!

UNLESS YOU BRING BACK THE SWORD, YOU WILL BE PUT TO THE RACK, BURNED AT THE STAKE AND BEHEADED!

BE-BE-HEADED?

The Black Knight was guarding the Singing Sword in a fortified castle. He was always ready to do battle – he never sent his suit to the cleaners, he just oiled the hinges. And in case any intruders broke in, he had a fiery dragon to make things hot for them.

8

But the dragon wasn't feeling very well. He had cold flushes, his temperature was low and he couldn't stop sneezing. And each sneeze was like a flame-thrower with hayfever.

The evil Knight could see that the dragon hadn't been eating properly, so he gave him a few shovelfuls of coal, just to keep him glowing.

When I arrived at the villain's castle, he was enjoying a bad knight's sleep, and the dragon was dozing, too. I tiptoed past them and made my way to the treasure chest where the Singing Sword was hidden.

As I took it out I breathed a sigh of relief – King Arthur wouldn't be parting this hare at the neck after all! But I still couldn't understand why there was such a fuss about this sword.

As I stole past the Knight, the Singing Sword started to live up to its name. The music woke the Black Knight who came after me with his axe. If he caught me, the live sabre would be the death of me!

I ran for the door and, since I didn't want the poor dragon's cold to get any worse, shut it behind me. That Black Knight can't have been very fit, because after that little run he was completely shattered!

Despite all this commotion the dragon had remained blissfully asleep, so the Black Knight decided it was time to stir his simmering hot-pet.

But the dragon was so dozy he didn't notice himself breathing fire all over his master until it was too late. The Black Knight's chops were grilled, his hams were smoked, and all of him was very tender!

I made my escape across the drawbridge and set off with the Singing Sword for Camelot. Suddenly I heard hoofbeats. The galloping dragon was gaining ground. The Black Knight wanted the sword back and

his motto was 'fry now, play later'.

The dragon's breath was making me a hot, cross bunny. I've always believed that the best way to get out of a hole is to go into one, so I borrowed a burrow while the dragon went past.

The Knight called for the dragon to stop.
He wasn't wearing a seat-belt, so when the
dragon stopped, the Black Knight didn't. He
got a bruise for every bump on the dragon's
back, and an extra one when he landed!

I knew I had to outwit the Knight or I'd never get the sword back to Camelot. So I ran back across the drawbridge and waited for him to set off again on the dragon. Then I raised the drawbridge.

WHOAH! WHOAH! ....
STUPID DRAGON.

The Black Knight yelled for the dragon to stop. You'd think that he'd have had the sense to belt up this time, but when the dragon stopped, he just kept going, right into the moat.

You don't expect cold, wet knights at this time of year, but there was one waiting for me under the drawbridge and he seemed very keen to meet me. Perhaps he hoped I had a crush on him. Well, I was flattered, but he was flattened.

My adversary had decided to spring a
surprise visit on me, so he used his dopey
dragon to pull a giant catapult to the bank
of the moat. He tried to launch himself
through the castle window and snatch back
the sword, but his aim wasn't quite good
enough. It was a near-miss but a nose-hit
as he flew smack into the wall and slid
down into the moat.

18

YOU'LL PAY FOR THIS, VARMINT!

Well, his armour may have been
dampened but his ardour wasn't. His next
plan was simple: lasso the battlements,
climb up the rope, and collar the rabbit.
It was so easy it seemed like bunny for old
rope. But even the best of plans can have
bugs in them!

The Black Knight seemed to be a keen
sportsman. He'd already played squash,
swum a length of the moat and told me I
was for the high-jump, so I thought he'd
be game for croquet.

He didn't know what hit him. Hadn't he

ever heard of a Knight-club?

The dazed knight clung on to the rope as his armour sank into the moat. It would be ruined by all that water, so he'd have to buy a new suit. After all, a change is as good as a rust.

The coast was clear, so my musicial mascot and I made our escape from the castle. We were going to race back to Camelot and have King Arthur rocking around the Round Table in no time.

But as we set off, I heard a roar like a boiler with 'flu in the flue. It was the dragon sneezing – and the Black Knight getting very hot under the collar.

AATCHOO!

OOWW! YOU IDIOT!

I ran back to the castle with the stormy
Knight close behind. The dragon was
coming too, but his nose was running faster
than his legs. Which was just as well,
because if he caught up with me he'd grill
this burglar with relish.

I fooled my pursuers into thinking I was hiding in a room full of explosives, then I crept out and locked them in.

The Black Knight kept all his explosives in one store-room: there were rolls of fuses, barrels of gunpowder, sticks of dynamite and tins of baked beans. He didn't plan it, but if the dragon sneezed he would set

alight the explosives. Then they'd both see stars, go into orbit and miss all the fun down on earth.

I had a terrible feeling that the dragon's
nose was starting to twitch, so I made a
quick getaway from the castle. Sure
enough, the sound of a sneeze was followed
by the roar of a massive explosion from the
North Tower. It didn't just rock it, it blasted
it into outer space – with the Black Knight
and his dim-witted dragon aboard.

26

It's a shame they didn't have time to pack
a picnic, but launch was a little early today!

Well, it's time to head back to Camelot.
I expect there will be celebrations afoot as
I inch across the yard with the Singing
Sword. I wonder who'll be sent to meet us.
Perhaps it'll be Sir Kit Breaker, the court
electrician, or Sir Gerry Hours, the palace
doctor.

Then we can all sit at the Round Table,
and eat and eat, until we've got Middle
Ages spread.

Except me of course – I've got to
entertain the King. Well, at least he won't
be feeling out-of-swords today!

Music, maestro . . .!